Perception Deception

R.G. Denbu

ISBN: 9798662741102

CONTENTS

Perception Deception

CHAPTER 1

The lampposts on the bridge flittered by as Harold eased into the backseat of his Uber. As always, his date went well. At this point in his online dating career, Harold had honed his routine to the level of a masterclass. He prided himself on the smooth machinations of each step, which lead to the inevitable climax: drinks at his favorite gastropub, a hole-in-the-wall frequented only by those in-the-know. Just the right level of obscurity made him appear as a cultured local, but not so much so that his date might suspect snobbery.

He would pull her seat out with practiced grace, and at a knowing glance, the bartender would send a bottle of Harold's preferred red to the table, in synchronicity. After seating her, Harold would glide to his own side of the table. Still, all the while blanked out, taking care to nod along at the right moments in their pointless conversation, murmuring approval or disbelief with a blithe disregard for his date's inane stories.

Having dated so many, he had familiarized himself with the full gamut of their complaints about work, love, and life. Without fail during each meal, his date would bleat about boys' pigheadedness. His trained ears honed in on the particular cadence of these complaints, always preceded by a long exasperated sigh and deep gulp from their wine. He waited for this flag each night, and like a hunter whose tripwire had snagged some tasty morsel, he would present his best mask of feigned grief, to conceal the instinctive yank of his face muscles pulling at the corners of his mouth into a sloping sneer. He would wince, almost as if in physical pain, at being implicitly associated with the dastardly dogs they bemoaned. The mask of wounded indignance would cause his dates to blush in embarrassment at having volleyed an insult at Harold, cueing him to prepare his coup de grâce.

It was the same each time, but nonetheless, his masterstroke. He would place his drink on the table, a third unfinished to show that she held his attention, reach across with both hands, and grasp her own delicate ones within his. Gazing into their eyes, he would say with a level of rehearsed finesse that even gave himself chills when he recited it in front of his mirror, "[Insert date's name], those are boys, and I'm a man.

I'll show you the difference tonight." It hadn't failed him yet--at that point, they were his. Despite his script feeling like greasing a well-worn groove, he liked to believe what he said.

Harold never thought of himself as a player, a fuck-boy, or whatever pejorative Twitter used to refer to his lesser competitors. No, none of those things. Harold considered himself a gentleman that privileged women with a good time and was thus rewarded for his charm and attentiveness with an inevitable invitation into their interior.

In the car, Harold engrossed himself in his phone. As his eyes glaze over in the universal sign of someone lost in a social media feed, something snaps him back to attention—an advertisement on VisageTome for a new dating app. Harold was always on the prowl for a new platform and relished the chance to fish in fresher waters. It advertised Blndr, the tagline enthusing: "Blind yourself to the distractions of normal dating apps! Puree your perceptions and blend your biases here! Let us auto-filter your photos so that dates see your inner self, and judge you by your dazzling personality, not your pseudo-enhanced looks! Try our patented new filter technology to get to the heart of the matter, not just the surface!"

Harold muttered as he scanned and scrolled through the terms and conditions, the legal lingo, and the rest of the B.S. "Yadda, yadda. User shall not hold BLNDR LLC liable for blah blah, permanent alterations...yuh huh ok right, perception of reality, and alterations thereof to the fabric of space...Ok, finally."

Harold groaned as the pages of text flashed by in a few moments, as he reached the checkbox at the bottom. Typing in his new Blndr bio, he wrote, "Chivalrous gentleman caught in a barbaric age. Seeking my one-and-only enchantress. Only a beautiful soul can break these shackles of the modern era that constrain me.' He nodded along as he reread and edited it down to a satisfactory state. Then, he added the obligatory taglines: 'My second home is the gym! If you don't live there too, please move on. P.S: No fatties, feminists, or LIBs need reply!" Satisfied with his bio, Harold leaned back with an outstretched arm and applied the grainy black-and-white filter, tilting his head in his most flattering angle, which he liked to think made him look both sincere and confident, and shot himself gazing out the window. *Perfect. Better than Bogart*, he thought.

Within minutes he got matches, and with a tactician's eye and technician's flick, he navigated the sea of profiles. Most were standard fare: bikini shots with dogs, friends at the club, hiking, and looking over a mountain range. 'How droll,' Harold thought as he passed judgment on each at blinding speed. From the blurred scroll of profiles, one leaped out: *Camilla.*

"Hell-loo," Harold purred as he clicked on her smiling face. A petite blonde from Texas beamed up at him, her profile as he preferred—succinct. Harold believed in all sincerity that any profile with over one paragraph of text was a catfish, and besides—who had time to read on dating apps? She only had a few photos, most of them modest, but he could tell from the obligatory black dress at the club pic that the girl was stacked. Even though she was short, she was thicccc, with a firm body (No visible belly bulge detected, excellent) and what looked like one hell of a rump. Her simple bio said:

'Howdy, y'all! 🤠 *Just a small-town girl from down South trying to make tracks in the Big* 🍎*. I'm a*

total foodie, and not one ***lick*** *shy about it. Take me for some BBQ, and you'll see I'm not afraid to get dirty. I'm a simple girl, take me to dinner, and I'll take you to the rodeo .*

Harold squirmed and panted in short lust-filled gulps in the back seat, writhing in appreciation of her profile. *This girl's spectacular! Just what I could use right now. A no-frills date with a quick release.* He added her, and within a few minutes, they matched on Blndr. Harold snapped off a speedy text to Camilla:

Howdy, baby. Are you ready to lasso this bucking bronco and be his reverse cowgirl? Let me show you the sweet juicy center of this city; just promise that you don't bite.

Harold read through the text and fired it off as he placed his phone down on his lap and waited for a reply. He looked down at his cellphone cockeyed, his displeasure clear on his face. *Fool!* He chastised himself as he grabbed his phone and opened the messenger again. Opening the emoji gallery with a sour twist on his mouth, how he hated these hieroglyphs of idiots, he looked for the right combination to translate his invitation:

Within a minute, he received a reply from Camilla:

Awwe! Ur such a sweaty! Yea lets meet up

Harold recoiled at her nauseating grammar. *Alas, such is the price I pay,* Harold thought with a solemn shake and lascivious grin. He rapped on the back of his driver's headrest. "Change of plans, take me to the theater on Greenvale and 4th—and make it snappy," Harold said while glancing at his phone. "I've got a hot date."

CHAPTER 2

He'd been standing in the theater's lobby for the better part of an hour, his patience sore as his knees. Less fortunate men waited on their dates, but Harold expected girls to wait on *him.* Harold considered leaving, but even he recognized such an idea as bravado.

An opportunity to witness beauty like Camilla's was tantalizing — enough to numb the aches in his joints, and almost sufficient to abate the nagging doubt slithering upon him. He rolled his shoulders again and craned his neck over the crowd's heads, hoping to spy a sliver of her sleek sandy hair.

He glanced at his phone and once more debated texting her, but caught himself once he remembered the first lesson his pickup coach drilled into him: *Alphas approach, Betas chase.*

He took a breath to steel himself, then placed his phone back into his pocket. In over two hundred dates, a girl had yet to ghost him. Camilla was gorgeous, but he knew she wouldn't be the first to crack that streak. He hoped. As he pushed his phone back into his pocket, he heard the distinct chime of a Blndr notification. *Score!*

Hey, cutie. Didnt find u in the lobby, but movie starting now. Lets meet inside if we can

Excellent. Don't worry, finding you will be easy. Your beauty will illuminate the path for me 😉

Inside, Harold let the crowd stream past him, scanning the faces for Camilla. After everyone took their seats, he still hadn't parsed her from the crowd. As the last of the moviegoers settled into their seats, Harold was despondent, standing alone in front of the screen. Was he being catfished?

"Hey, moron! Siddown in the front! Yer blockin' the screen you knobhead!" Bellowed a middle-aged man wearing an overtaxed Star Wars shirt. Unperturbed, Harold turned to face the slope of seats behind him, a confident hip cocked. His posture radiated condescension as he prepared to lambast his detractor. Before he could retort, the man ended the discussion by hurling a half-drunk "thirst-throttler" at him with a perfect spiraling arc. Harold scuttled to the nearest front-row seat with an undignified yelp and crunched himself into it to reduce the likelihood of his head being pelted further by sugary artillery.

Now seated, his phone wedged itself tight in his jean's diminutive pocket, and prying it out gave his hand friction burns. "*Why can't Italian designers make anything fashionable* and *functional?*" he griped to himself. He cupped a hand around the screen to reduce the glow and not show his position. Blndr showed a new message:

Couldn't find u. Im in the back, but lets meet in the lobby by the snack stand

Harold's heart soared as he typed a response:

I'll order the sweetest treat they have, and it will still pale compared to your smile 😘

The movie was a typical summer blockbuster-trite. Harold recorded his series of critiques, both technical and creative, to impress Camilla with his discerning taste. *Is she more of a Bergman or Kubrick fan?* He pondered while strolling over to the snack stand. He leaned against the counter with his eyes on the river of people as they streamed out. The vendor behind the counter slunk up to Harold's back.

"Hey, pal! Can I interest you in our newest menu item—the Double-Dipper Triple-Wide Bounty Bucket?" asked the attendant. Harold deigned to give the briefest over-the-shoulder glance to the balding soda-jerk. Misinterpreting Harold's glower as a sign of interest, he continued his pitch. "Or maybe I could interest you in a thirst-throttler? They come in large, extra-large, and our newest size, hydrant," the clerk informed.

"Hydrant?" Harold asked despite himself, turning toward the man.

Desperate for a sale, and sensing an opportunity, the jerk perked. "Yes, sir! Just recently approved by the FDA, our hydrant size has 33% more soda than any other legally available drink receptacle—Two. Hundred. Fifty. Six. Ounces! That's two gallons of Fizzy Sissy, Gassy Guzzler, Crank Cola, or Burper Beer, if that's your thing. We don't judge here," the sugar-hyper man rattled off his pitch with the blistering haste of an auctioneer.

The sugar-peddler's offerings revolted Harold. "You hawk off literal bucketfuls of diabetes to people, and the only people buying this garbage are the ones with ticking bombs for hearts. How do you sleep knowing you dole out sugar-dipped death sentences?" Harold demanded. His face contorted into a twisted sneer, which he leveled at the man behind the counter like a loaded gun. If looks could kill, then Harold's would ensure the candy-man would sling his last soda this day.

Either the soda-jerk developed a tolerance for such tirades through inundation or didn't comprehend Harold's words. To his credit, he maintained a professional decorum, and his eager smile never slid.

"Just doing my job, sir. People lo-oove a fresh bucketful of pop or a couple of dozen deep-fried cheese logs, but I understand if you're more health-conscious. Here at the Coldwell Center Theater, we accommodate all lifestyles and dietary fads. How about something greener?" asked the clerk as he ducked behind the counter and began rummaging out of sight in a clatter. He rose back before Harold, holding an enormous ovular loaf of bread. "How about one of our classic bread bowls? We hollow this baby out, pump it to the brim with velvety cheese, and then toss in a healthy dollop of baby broccoli and macaroni. Then we seal it up in some batter, and dunk it in our patented frying grease, which might I add, is available wholesale," he said as he jerked a thumb over his shoulder to the display behind the counter.

Upon the shelves, Harold saw a sequence of mason jar quarts filled with an opaque ochre grease. Each jar adorned with a sticker label of the man's face beaming an insane toothy grin down at Harold's own, horrified. If looks could kill, then Harold was out-manned and outgunned by the firing squad behind the counter.

Harold found no words for the odd little man, so instead, he elected to turn his back on the snack-stand and dismiss the jerk with a curt wave of his hand, looking back into the crowd.

Gathering in the lobby's heart, the attendees were a ball of energy. Harold's eyes flitted from face to face in search of Camilla. He observed coquettish women giggling as they swatted at their dates in faux-offense; listened in on fervent fans debating how this latest sequel changed the canon of the fictional universe; couples discussing last-minute dinner plans for the local diner.

Harold stuck around in the lobby waiting for Camilla to glide through the gate and into his arms. Still, as ten minutes turned to twenty, his insecurities swarmed his confidence, cannibalizing it.

Where is she? Did I really get stood up? He struggled with the question and its implications, working it over like a sour morsel wedged in his teeth.

Bolts of tension jolted throughout his body, overloading his already frazzled nerves. His foot drummed out a legato tempo on the soda-stuck floor of the snack stand, his nails scritch-scratched out a sequence of accompanying notes across his jeans, and his grinding jaw clicked out the occasional 'pop!'. Soon enough, his anxiety orchestrated a cacophony of scrapes, taps, and clicks, coalescing into a rhythm and melody—an original theme from "*Harold and the Bruised Egos.*"

"Hey! Watch it!" shouted a man from the depths of the crowd.

Some immense thing was plodding through, forcing the meandering masses to thin. Harold gawked at the spectacle, hearing the gasps and complaints of the trampled and fleeing bystanders. They scattered, bodies swaying like bramble underfoot of a large predator. He felt like a hunted rabbit in a clearing, lacking the reason to listen to his gut, which urged him to leave. It stamped in a relentless drive toward the edge of the crowd, prepared to burst out and pounce in a snarling fury.

They surged, tripping over one another to accommodate the blazing path of the beast in their midst. Without warning, it blasted a splayed opening through the mass of the human wall, sending bodies tumbling and flailing. From the opening emerged an absolute behemoth of blubber who had just moments ago cleaved through the throng of people with the same indifference as a steel maul splitting a rotted pumpkin caught in its crescent. She loomed, as a conqueror, over the trail of human wreckage her path had wrought. The crumbled crowd akin to a sacked city. Unaware, or indifferent to the people's plight, she gulped air with as much gluttony as she did everything else.

"Good Lord! Leave some for the rest of us, or we may all die of oxygen deprivation," Harold muttered in awe at the sight of such a hog.

Once her deep whooping breaths leveled off, she was on the move again. To no one's surprise, she swayed, shimmied, bumped, barreled, waddled, and wobbled her way over the final stragglers to the snack stand. In her thundering wake, she left bodies sprawled across the floor. Women wailed, and men glowered with unconcealed spite at her broad, bouncing behind as they bent to help their trampled dates.

Her alien dimensions evoked equal amounts of fascination and repulsion through the spectacle of her singular migration. Her body was a marvel the same way that Chernobyl or a beached whale carcass was—terrifying in scope, and even more harrowing to behold in person. She, a titan of flesh, must be 300—no, ***at leas*t** 400 pounds by Harold's estimate.

Despite her enormity, she was adorned in a stylish crimson sheath dress. Its tight seams outlined her drooping gut, and the hemline receded quicker than the polar icecaps as she waddled, revealing her grotesque jiggling thighs. A fashionisto, Harold immediately recognized it as a Badgely Mischka, but he knew there was no possibility she got it off-the-rack. It must have been a custom fit for someone as fat as her. Clearly, this woman had connections, or money, probably both.

Harold trembled in dread and outrage that any designer would be so deranged to permit this woman to disgrace such a design. It subjected bystanders to the full expanse of the voluminous columns of her legs—and *that* was unacceptable. Her lumbering girth was a burden that well exceeded what nature intended a human skeleton to carry, as shown by the draping folds cascading off her legs to the ground. Harold's imagination strained to its limits imagining the normal-sized frame encased within that suit of adipose, like a candle's wick in its tallow prison.

Lines, creases, pockets, divots, dimples, and ridges merged into a topographical texture across her quivering trotters. The diversity of shapes and textures across her legs reminded him of the globe that obsessed him in grade-school. How he loved running his tiny palms across its surface, teasing out the bumps which represented mountains and continents, marveling that such slight lumps served vast structures.

Rushing along with her thigh's undulating geography was an extensive series of stretch marks; river channels carved out a weaving path along with the bases of the cellulite mountains over many years. Her thighs were so replete with swaths of cellulite that they formed a latticework that was intricate enough to shame any artisan. *Proof patterns can develop from randomness; or at least cheeseburgers.*

It was self-evident that she was ill-suited to walking, and yet despite her pace being an agonizing crawl, her progress was steady. That she could continue to throw one mammoth leg forward and around the other spoke to incredible strength. Anyone could see how her exertion produced a secretion of slick sweat, which coated her wobbling thighs. *It might even work as a natural lubricant for chaffing,* Harold theorized with a restrained gag.

Studying her legs further, he noticed an omission of two essential joints. *Where are her knees?!* Harold's mind became unhinged as he searched for them. He found two dimpled ridges where her knees *should* have been. Still, her thighs had annexed that territory in a campaign of expansion, rendering it impossible to distinguish where the border terminated between thigh and calf. Her titanic form tottered on doughy feet that rose like half-baked loaves over the edges of her ballet flats, scuffling along the floor in whispering scrapes.

Enthralled by her enormous lower half, he neglected to notice her sustained lumbering descent upon the snack stand. She loomed larger as she waddled ever closer. Like Godzilla storming towards an unsuspecting Tokyo, he expected there would be no survivors found after her arrival. He hoped her appetite for saturated sugar was more sizable than her penchant for destruction.

His eyes climbing, he saw the jutting edges of her hips rise and fall in an asynchronous rhythm. *Is that her ass—coming out past the front?* Her hips jiggled in a mesmerizing motion, and he was soon studying their peculiar pattern. Raise the left, lower the right, clench, wobble, release, reverse, repeat.

Before he realized it, she stood beside him, fanning herself with a sausage-fingered hand, causing the hanging grain sacks under her arms to swing back and forth. Long after she stopped, they continued to wobble under their own weight. She began tapping away a message with nimble fingers that belied her girth.

CHAPTER 3

A ping in his pocket broke his slack-jawed enthrallment. *My sweet Camilla, save me by purging the sight of this abomination.* He unlocked his phone and read Camilla's text:

Here! At the snack stand. I don't see u 🙁

Harold grinned as he replied:

I'm leaning on the counter by the register. Look for me again, my sweet.

How did I miss her? The moment after hitting send, the familiar tinkling chime of Blndr pinged nearby. *She's close!* Knowing it must be her, he whipped toward the source like a hooked fish being reeled. Again, the enormous woman blocked his view, her immensity surging against the edge of the counter, flowing over the top, as she typed on her phone.

He stared at her profile, studying, trying to reconcile the strange series of events: her elephantine ass, spreading against the glass surface; the sagging U-shaped belly's outline which covered her crotch and snagged folds of her dress around its edges; bare arms, swaddled in hanging fat which hung and swung in wobbling sacks whenever she lifted one to brush aside an errant bang or take a selfie; moon-crater thighs which forced her to assume a gunslinger's stance and penguin's waddle; her dumpling-shaped face, with the ring of fat encircling her neck like a choker—the perfect white teeth framed by full sensual red lips, allusions of high and angular cheekbones buried beneath mounds of fat on her cheeks, the delicate nose centered between her glorious emerald eyes, and luminous golden blonde hair, cut short just like... Camilla's.

Without warning, the sticky theater floor crumbled beneath him, pieces falling into a stretching void, the null space between worlds. Now he followed their trail into the inky obsidian darkness, tumbling into oblivion with no sense of direction. Gloom enveloped him, folded over him in infinite layers until he became insensate. Plunged into this desolate abyss, he surrendered all sense of self, his body and mind sundered from one another as his flesh sloughed off, his bones clattering away into unknowable reaches. Just a dim flicker of consciousness bobbling along in the dark. Here he ceased being part of the world, with its rules and logic—he existed in this place, at peace in this null space.

With the same abruptness as he entered the space, it vaulted him back into his body, layer by layer. Back in the theater, standing by the snack stand, something… pliable, swaddled him. It smothered him, crushing the air from his lungs, the desire from his loins, the will from his existence.

The enormous girl wrapped her arms around his waist, pressing her stomach against his torso as far as possible. Sensing his stiffness, she looked up to study his face. She quirked her mouth with a curious tilt and knotted her immaculate brows in consternation.

"Harold, right?" she asked. Her voice was sultry as a balmy beach breeze. Harold's body stiffened again in an unexpected and distressing manner, albeit beyond his control.

"Uh, yes? I'm Harold. Are you?—"

"Camilla," she chirped, nodding. Her face sloshed like a water-balloon with the movement. Unclenching him from her marshmallow embrace, she steered herself back in a wobbling step to survey him. Harold did the same.

Despite the blatant disparities, Camilla was the same girl from her Blndr pictures. Sort of.

Beneath the obfuscation of hundreds of pounds, Harold saw the same pearish figure from the pictures, just… ripened, and her face—unblemished skin, perfect white teeth, and those emerald eyes—too bright, too verdant, to be someone else's. *I'm convinced that's her, but have I really been waiting all night for this fatty?! What happened? Is the picture of her sister? It's impossible to have gained so much weight, right?...*

She trained her sights upon him, studying him in equal measure. Her luminous eyes shone in her round spongy face; two pristine emeralds sunk deep into a greedy mound of baker's dough. Despite being cloaked by so much fat, her eyes held an astute gleam that made Harold uncomfortable. The ring of fat under her chin creased as the jowls flanking her pursed mouth folded into a frown, a mirror of Harold's own disappointment.

To avoid her scrutinizing gaze, Harold avoided meeting her eyes and instead cast his own below hers. Surveying her body, Harold strained to locate her breasts. When he thought he found them, he couldn't be sure what they were. Shaped like they were, two drooping scoops of melting ice cream, the flabby pair camouflaged themselves among tiers of other rolls and folds—many of which were several degrees larger than her actual breasts. Even by a normal woman's proportions, they were small, but in juxtaposition to her battleship-class hips, ass, and everything else, having such diminutive folds for breasts was a cruel genetic irony as if they were an afterthought. *Poor girl.* Harold shook his head in solemn recognition of her physical shortcomings.

Steeling himself, Harold understood the situation with perfect clarity. Because of a pairing of negligent life choices and an insidious genetic blueprint, Camilla had condemned herself to a literal confinement of her own flesh—warden and prisoner both.

She catfished because she was desperate for a date. Tragic. I must show this pudge-pile a good night regardless of how revolting her obesity is. She chose me, and not only because I'm handsome, but because all women know I'm a cut above the rest. Harold nodded to himself, his chivalrous duty superseding his withering libido as the motivator of the night.

"Hm," Camilla said, cocking her hip to the side as she swung her titanic weight from foot to foot. She flopped one drooping grain-sack arm across her chest, resting it on the crest of her belly's uppermost bulge. She nestled a plump hand into the creased crook of her elbow, the candy-apple red nails peeking out the other side. With her other hand, she placed a painted sausage to the corner of her mouth, thinking.

"Something wrong, my dear?" Harold asked in his best impression of a man not on the verge of losing his sanity.

"We-lll," she held the final syllable to collect her thoughts. "It's just that, and I'm NOT superficial, but you're much shorter than you said on your profile," she said while evaluating.

Looking him up and down sent her sub-chins wobbling in mock affirmation of her assessment like a trio of doughy yes-men. Shifting her weight once more with an oceanic undulation across her body, she took a step toward Harold. Her gut was unyielding as it forced a sharp grunt from him. She leaned closer, pinning him against the counter, studying his face, her pursed painted lips red as a stop sign. At that moment, Harold realized with a rushing sense of dread that despite being a foot taller than her and in significantly better shape, she eclipsed him in physical stature. The pressure of her weight on him was a threat to his own ego, and regardless if it was another man or his own morbidly obese date, Harold wouldn't let anyone size him up and push him around. He glowered at her, twin twinkling jades buried in the fat folds, a jeering glint visible.

She's testing me! Harold's mind reeled. *How's a tub like her not intimidated by* ***me?*** In Harold's expectations, validated by years of such experience, women yielded to his self-confidence, not challenged him. Of all the dates he had wined, dined, and enjoyed supine, no one had ever given him a look like Camilla did now—quiet dominance, which posed a challenge to the agreed-upon social hierarchy with Harold perched above all others.

Harold tried to rise to his full height, intending to tower above Camilla and look down on her, but as he attempted to climb from his casual slouch on the counter, it forced him to grapple with an opponent far beyond his weight class: her gut. His arms trembled from the strain as he shoved against the veritable wall of flesh. What started with Harold hoping to gain leverage or relief, became a wrestling match in which his loss risked her fatness consuming him. Sickened by her sucking blubber and mortified to recognize that Camilla's crushing weight was more than he could lift, it humiliated him to submit to her.

Her pressing folds on his chest forced him to lean further back on the counter, hoping to salvage his ribs and lungs from being crumpled under her heft, being forced to his ego behind to be crushed beneath her. Being rendered helpless as a rabbit in a wolf's jaw enraged him. Domination was as unfamiliar to him as diet soda was to her.

His bulging eyes burned with a smoldering fury as they fixated on her taunting smirk bracketed by bulbous cheeks. Camilla met Harold's burning hateful eyes with her own calculating and dispassionate gaze. After a few moments, it calmed him, her focus somehow dousing his anger. Unperturbed by the exchange, she giggled, as light and resonant as a chime tinkling in a gentle breeze, and so concluded the tense exchange with an arbiter's finality.

"You're cute, I'll give you that—little boy," the quip stressed with a long-lashed wink.

She began steering her bulk in reverse. Harold felt the burn in his chest from having to hold his breath, but he still refused to suck the sweet, refreshing air his lungs howled to taste. To do so would show weakness, he decided, and thus he maintained a debonair smirk on his face while surreptitiously sucking in air from the corner of his mouth. His chest ached, but it was difficult to say which was more bruised from Camilla's display—his ribs or ego. *Fat bitch!* his mind screeched in rage. *I underestimated this warthog.*

"Yes, well, I believe there may have been... misrepresentations on both parts in our profile, it's fair to say," Harold said from behind his teeth-shattering tight smile. Camilla quirked her head at Harold's words, wry amusement and curiosity flitted across her face.

"Let's get something to eat. I'm *starved* after that movie," Camilla said without a trace of irony. Harold was gobsmacked. Taking her out to eat would disgust him, if not bankrupt him. *But I have a duty,* he reminded himself.

"I can only imagine how hungry you must be," he said, clearing his throat before adding "wouldn't want you to waste away."

Her reply was more musical laughter before swinging her bulk against him, throwing a massive wobbling cheek into his groin. "How thoughtful," she purred. "Harry, you're *tall*," she said, her tone carrying an undercurrent of mocking mirth. "Look over the crowd. Find the bathroom for me? If you can. I'm so short and *petite* that I couldn't make it through this crowd on my own," she said, emphasizing with a staggering thrust of her butt that almost knocked him to the floor.

"It's Harold," he corrected her with a terse edge behind his tight smile while trying to lean away from her quivering backside. "Let me find it for you," he said while stealing a sly peek to make sure she wasn't looking. Confident that her eyes were elsewhere, he stretched to his full height, leaning forward on his toes for the few extra inches he needed to see over the top of the packed lobby. Spotting the sign for the Women's room, he points over her head. "That way. Should I wait for you here?" he asked. With a final back-thrust into Harold followed by a gyrating shimmy of flesh, she takes her first laborious step forward.

"I think you should go and, ahem, clean yourself up as well before dinner, Harry," she informs him. Her eyebrow cocked above a discerning emerald darting in Harold's direction. Mortified, he drops his heels flat to the ground, hoping that she didn't see his inability; but as she begins her slow shuffle off towards the bathroom, he realizes she wasn't looking at his feet.

Aside from his height, his body had betrayed him in another, more unexpected, way. The bulge nudging against his zipper siphons the strength from his knees, and he rushes to the Men's room on wobbling uncertain legs to "adjust" himself. *It could happen to anyone,* he reassured himself. *It was a lot of motion and stimulation down there, it wasn't because of her!* He pleaded with himself to believe such logic, but a nagging suspicion couldn't be abated.

Inside the bathroom, Harold sequestered himself inside the first available stall. Perched on the toilet, he took a moment to orient himself. Opening the Blndr app on his phone, he studied Camilla's profile once more. *This isn't some "gotcha" set up with a hidden camera, right?* As he considered the likelihood, he overheard a conversation by the sinks.

"—just enormous, man. I'm telling you, that hog just barreled through us like she didn't care," one man recounted his experience with the tone of disbelief reserved for survivors of natural disasters or armed combat.

"Probably couldn't slow down. Someone that big moves with momentum. And **goddamn**, did you see her ass hanging out the bottom of that dress? Just nasty, dude. I want to see the guy who brought her here tonight," a second voice replied, followed by a peeling snicker.

The mocking guffaw bounced along the tiled walls and landed in Harold's stall like an artillery shell falling into his lap. Harold's face burned with humiliation. If anyone he knew saw him with Camilla in public, it would wreck his image beyond repair. The people in the lobby must have seen them talking—by the snack stand no less! *How mortifying.* Harold pushed the stall door open with a gentle creak and kept his eyes on the floor as he maneuvered to the sink like he was navigating a minefield. He felt the two men's eyes on him, no doubt trying to sleuth out why he looked familiar. Harold dried his hands and slipped out of the bathroom before they could figure it out.

Camilla sat on a bench outside, scrolling through her phone while occupying its entirety with her yard-wide ass. A group of women clustered a few feet away huddled and gossiping while taking turns to gawk at the jiggling mountain that was his date for the night.

Harold sidled over next to her and nudged an aqueous hip pouring over the side to get her attention. "Harry, get me up. Then let's head for the buffet," she commanded while scrolling on her phone. He refused, there was no way. Clearing his throat, he offered an outstretched hand, palm upward. With one thick eyebrow curved in wry amusement, she looked up from her phone. "Harry," she said in a stern voice, "I need you to help me get up, so give me both hands and use your knees."

Now Harold started to sweat. She wouldn't concede. The gaggle of women giggled behind their hands, except one who cast aside such social niceties and succumbed to a sequence of uproarious honking. He knew it was only a matter of time before they recorded this if they weren't already. Having this circulated online would be the end of his dating life, and having his last date be with her was a fate worse than death.

Having calculated the mental calculus of social media's potential to damage his e-dating persona, he stepped in front of Camilla, both hands outstretched. She placed each of her plump hands in his, and he clutched around her spongey wrists. *Like squeezing brioche.* Leaning back, he hoped to serve as a counter-weight and aid in the slow liftoff from the launchpad of her bench. With a wet sucking pop, which Harold realized with a lurch was the sweat-slick pocketed craters of her ass adhering to the stone top of the seat, she was upright. She loosed a girlish yelp as she came to her feet. Harold had misjudged his own placement when offering to help her up because now that she was on her feet again, she stood on top of him, her jiggling body pressed against his, eclipsing it. He leaped back, fearful it would look like they were embracing. Panting from the exertion of Harold lifting her, she placed a gentle hand on his chest and made a small circle over his pec.

"Mm. I love a firm man," she said with a flash of that perfect smile. Harold didn't think a compliment could induce nausea, but it was a night of many firsts. Nonetheless, her hand on his chest elicited a strange tingling thrill.

"Come now, Harry. Let's stop by 'The Greasy Though.' I'm starved," she said with emphasis directed over Harold toward the women no doubt eavesdropping from across the lobby. Their catty cackles were death-by-thousand-cuts for Harold.

Harold had booked a table in advance at his usual place in the Village, but towing this tanker into his stomping ground was an affront liable to get him banned. The thought alone of those careening hips navigating through the narrow aisles of "Gregorio's" was enough to make him cringe. Grateful to avoid the shame, he conceded to Camilla's demand they go to the local all-night greasy-spoon buffet.

"Whatever you want, Camilla," he said, pushing her along from behind toward the exit.

"You're learning. Good," she said, permitting Harold to maneuver her.

CHAPTER 4

Their Uber crawled into the entrance of "The Greasy Trough", announcing their arrival with a scraping drag toward the rear. Harold stared out the window from the front passenger seat in marvel. Having lived his entire life in the city, he had never seen a feeding trough for hogs on a farm, but at once knew the name for this slop-house was àpropos.

And although it had a distinct farm theme with workers wearing bib overalls, and patrons feasting from steel-bucketed trays while resting their bulk on literal hay bales, he couldn't help but see it as more akin to a cargo loading bay than the entrance to a restaurant. The opening didn't use doors, but an open rectangular dock with a collapsed steel shutter above it. Harold could just imagine the manager yanking on the chain pulley in a rattling procession as the shutter clattered open each morning at 7.

As he studied the odd species of land-whales lumbering toward the sloped handicap-accessible ramps to either side, he understood the need for the entrance's design. They kept their enormous quavering forms upright by the reinforced handrails, and for those true flesh titans, they whirred along on motorized platforms with armrests, which used wheels thick as truck tires. He half expected to see tarmac attendants waving them on with a series of elaborate hand gestures, glowing cones, and whistles.

Feeling the SUV rock about like a HotWheels, he knew that Camilla was getting antsy, and that meant he'd have to aid in her extrication. He looked over to the driver in a feeble hope that he'd offer to help, but the man stared forward in silence, his white-knuckled grip on the wheel as clear a message as Harold needed: *'Don't even ask,'* it said.

After a few tries, Harold had as good a hold as he could manage on Camilla's puffy wrists. In a series of synchronized tugs, she surged out of the backseat like canned biscuit dough left to sit in the heat bursting from its confines. She levied her weight on him, panting as she raised the back of her hand to pat her slick forehead.

"Mmm. You sure are strong, Harry, but you will have to bulk up soon to be a match for me," she purred in his ear as she nuzzled her water-balloon cheek into the crook of his neck. Her breath was sharp as a dagger as it cut into his nostrils with undertones of butter and chocolate—no doubt, she had gorged plenty at the theater. Her words revolted him almost as much as the damp perfumed humidity that emanated off of her.

Harold sidestepped in haste around her, reaching for the door and slamming it shut, but it bounced back on its hinge with force. He tried again, but it kept meeting with the same spongy resistance. Looking past her into the car, he realized with revulsion that even though most of her bulk had cleared the backseat, her enormous elephantine ass still lingered a disturbing distance into the vehicle. It wobbled with a residual rubbery sway from the car door slamming it.

"There's a lot back there, babe," she tittered before walking off to join the others in the queue at the loading dock entrance.

Harold glanced at the driver, hoping to share in a moment of camaraderie, but from his rigid posture alone, Harold knew they felt the same. He would have to leave him a decent tip as compensation for the damage to his car's suspension.

He joined Camilla in the lumbering line at the ramp, trying to keep his distance from her to avoid association. That only lasted for a minute before another enormous couple shimmied up behind him, gabbling in excitement about the "cornbread-by-the-sheet-pan deal." One of their sloping boulder-bellies crashed into Harold, launching him forward. *Damned belly-brutes!* He lambasted the couple behind him as he reeled from the unsolicited prod. The shock unbalanced him, sending him shambling into Camilla's jiggling backside. Sticking his hands out from reflex caused him to slip one arm around Camilla's flank, plunging it between the rolls where her love handle flowed onto her hip, and the other planted firm on the swatch of half-exposed cellulite-coated thigh-ass. He pulled back from her rolling body in horror and spied the swiveling profile of her face, one long-lashed emerald eye glittering in sneering amusement.

"Easy, *big boy,*" she said with a quaking shimmy that caused the hem of her dress to inch up a nauseating amount. She pinched the hem and yanked it down, before turning back around, oblivious that it scrunched again over the curve of her cheek's crease back to its earlier position.

The line moved at a glacial pace, and Harold had the distinct feeling of being in a corral. The bovine bodies around him only added to the sensation as they shuffled their weight on aching feet and knees, snorting in exhaustion, and jostling against one another. He expected them to moo at any moment.

Nearing the front of the line, Harold could see an employee at a podium ushering guests inside. The attendant, a teenage girl, had been working here long enough to resemble the clientele. Her uniform, outgrown bib overalls, stretched without mercy over a prodigious corn-fed body all her own. Harold ruminated on the colloquialism "poured into an outfit," and thought she brought new meaning to the term. He couldn't imagine another way the poor girl pulled those straps on other than being liquefied and funneled in like a baker's mold. Her moon-face beamed a bright smile as they closed the distance.

"Howdy, y'all!" she said, shouting into their faces.

Harold recoiled, but returned her smile, albeit with much more strain. "Hi…" he said, leaning in to read the name tag pinned above one of the brass buttons, it said "Stacey." "Hi, Stacey," he repeated. "We'd like...", looking over at Camilla, "a booth, please."

"First time?" She asked with a gleeful wobble.

"Definitely for me, not so much her, obviously," he jerked a thumb over his shoulder at Camilla the way one would point at a natural landmass or equivalent immobile structure.

Camilla surged forward, sending Harold stumbling aside with a devastating jerk of belly and hip. "Gimme two bales and a stool for the little guy. Kay, sweetie?" Camilla said as she lumbered into the restaurant, not waiting to hear Stacey's reply.

"Um, right away, Miss!" Stacey called after her. Then she pulled a walkie-talkie out of a cavernous pocket on her belly pouch and chattered into it with urgency. Trailing behind Camilla, he overheard Stacy's communications on her radio. "Big C. coming in hot! Headed toward table 8—new date in tow…" she whispered in clipped commands.

Camilla walked to the nearest clean table and rapped one pudgy knuckled fist on its surface, emitting a sharp, albeit fat-muffled report throughout the restaurant. In a matter of moments, two enormous men scrambled to their table. One wielded a thick iron hook in each hand, plunged into two dense saffron-colored rectangles of hay. The other carried a simple bar-stool. The first slid the two bales together lengthwise, creating a four-foot-long surface, which Camilla plopped upon. Her cheeks and hips threatened to surge over the sides despite the inhuman square footage.

From the theater to the table, the flurry of events left him stunned. *How was it possible for a human to look, let alone behave like Camilla?* Yet here he was in this den of gluttony, surrounded by more of her kind. *Where did such enormous monstrosities hide during the day*? He wondered.

He flinched and recoiled as herds of them stomped down the mile-wide aisles, the foundation-shaking steps overtures of their arrival. Orbital bellies, breasts, and butts shifted and sloshed as they bumped and bashed through the restaurant, carried by trajectories they were beholden to—the hot buckets of fried foods baking under the heat lamps at the buffet line. And across the table from him, was Camilla, so comfortable here among her subjects, exuding a confidence befitting regality. With spite and awe, he leered at her, the fat of her arms pooling at her elbows across the table as she studied him through the steeple of her fingers.

"Don't stare, Harry—it's rude," she chastised him again in that distinct headmistress tone.

Harold snapped his eyes to the table, staring at his hands, through the knife-and-fork-scarred wood, fumbling underneath. Why was he so nervous? *I'm a catch in standard company, but among this Dionysian feasting hall, I'm Adonis.* He cleared his throat and sat straight.

"So, Camilla…" he said before realizing he hadn't the faintest idea how to talk to this woman. If she was a catfish, was everything else a lie? He slid his eyes up to meet hers, for the first time since the theater. He was misled by his foolish assumption that her size implied she would be humble, and yet she never once played at even the pretense of vulnerability. *No, she's a spider, and I think I've been caught in something.* As he studied her from across the table, he wondered: *The question is, just how big is this web?*

"Yes, Harry? You were saying?" she asked, her eyes fastened to him.

"Um," he fumbled for words while Camilla's eyes were punching into him. They gave him the feeling she could see his squirming discomfort. "What do you do? For work," he asked. He was sweating from the effort of asking.

"Oh," she fluttered her hand in a dismissive arc like a bird too fat to fly, and too pampered to bother trying. "Banking. Very dry. I'm sure you wouldn't really understand it," she said.

Harold became incensed at her implication, but in a way relieved, he had an out to pivot away from the conversation. Regardless, he refused to allow her to intimidate or humiliate him anymore tonight. He was here taking *her* on a date, *she* should be grateful for it. "Oh, I'm sure it's fascinating," he countered. "Please, indulge me--"

A card swished across the table toward him, twirling before slowing to a stop. *When did she?"* He picked the card up, forced to acknowledge the cardstock had a premium thickness and texture. Running his finger over the embossed header, which read "*Coldwell Bank,"* followed by "Camilla Coldwell." Harold trembled, and his face must have betrayed his recognition as he dragged his eyes up toward her smirk.

"*That* Coldwell, yes," she said. "You probably have an account with us even. Statistically speaking, we serve most of the city," she said.

Harold *did* have an account with Coldwell. His life savings were in a branch around the corner from his house. *Is that significant? What does it mean that I'm on a date with the heiress of my bank?*

"Like I said, *so* boring," she said before raising her hand and snapping at the nearest worker.

A portly man waddled over much quicker than Harold assumed possible. "Yes, Ms. Coldwell? How can I help you today?" he asked from behind an empty serving tray he held flat against his chest, reminiscent of an elephant hiding behind a pebble.

"You," she said, pointing a ruby finger at the cowering attendant who flinched behind his tray further like it was a gun, "take *him," jerking a* thumb at Harold, "and help him bring me back a tray. Kay? Good." She took her phone out and scrolled.

Fire licked at his cheeks. *Who does this fat bitch think she is? Just because she owns a* few *banks?* Harold's stool screeched as the legs scraped the floor, causing the cowering attendant to jump in a thundering clap. "Hold on--" before he could finish, someone hooked Harold's arm with a meaty paw, dragging him off in a frenzy. If Camilla noticed Harold's outburst, she showed nothing as she focused on her phone.

Harold was being ushered off toward the enormous steel trays where the food passed through a series of large chutes. The man was panting when they stopped at the edge, cutting ahead of the line of furious feasters. "Please! I don't know how you met Miss. Coldwell, but believe me, it's best not to challenge her," the man huffed.

Hands clenched in a fury, Harold spun on his heel to look up at the tomato-faced man. "Who the hell is she? What's going on?" Harold demanded.

The man's doughy face creased in fear. "C'mon, she likes lobster, crab, and Mac'nCheese," he said over his shoulder as he moved over to the serving tables. Placing his hefty tray down, he grabbed one of the mammoth chutes and shifted it over with a grunt. "Pull that lever there by the side," he jerked his head to a series of buttons, knobs, and pull-handles.

Harold stared at the contraption, baffled why a buffet needed such industrial grade machinery. Leaving such questions unanswered, Harold gripped the handle, compressing the hand-grip, which resulted in a pneumatic hiss of steam as he struggled to engage the lever. As he did, the chute the man held rattled and rocked, a waterfall of macaroni floating in steaming neon-yellow cheese sluiced out in a wet splatter on the plate. The man held a hand, palm out, toward Harold, and after the plate was half full, he sliced his hand through the air. Harold released the lever, which sprang back. The chute clattered and groaned under the burden of cheesy pasta before the final dregs slopped out at the end onto the plate. Harold's horror and revulsion were short-lived when he heard the collective moaning and lowing of those still waiting in line. Their eyes glazed with animalistic yearning directed at the mountain of steaming gold.

"Here! Hurry, Harry!" the man waved from another titanic table, pulling down another chute.

"What's your name? Who are you?" Harold asked.

"Me? I'm nobody, just another proud employee of 'The Greasy Trough", but you can call me Daryll," Daryll said, offering his hand for Harold.

Harold took the man's hand in his, trying to ignore the sticky coating of powdered cheese and cream sauce remnants. "So why are you so afraid of Camilla?" Harold asked. The man jerked his head once again at the lever system next to Harold. "Oh, right. Sorry," Harold engaged the lever, and a similar rocking clatter of movement shook the chute as dozens of King Crab legs thunked down onto the plate.

"You're on a first-name basis with Miss Coldwell already? You must have really caught her eye, Harry," Daryll said while fighting against the enormous force of the chute spewing the girthiest crab legs Harold had ever seen.

All of this tiptoeing around Camilla exasperated Harold. Daryll would not give him any more information, but whether he meant to, the fear in his eyes told Harold enough—there was something dangerous about her. Once Camilla's tray was overflowing with shellfish and processed pasta Daryll thrust it over to Harold and scooted him back to the table.

Harold tottered under the tray's weight and made his way back toward Camilla on unsteady legs.Her eyes tracked him along the serving area back to the table, and throughout, they bore into him through the mountain of food laid before her. For all his bluster and frustration with his date throughout the night, his rebellion wilted under her oppressive focus. Daryll watched him from the depths of the crowd, and said a silent prayer for Ms. Coldwell's date, hoping that he didn't end up like the others.

Harold dropped the food on the table in front of Camilla without ceremony. The table groaned and swayed under its extra burden, but held steady. "Here's your food," Harold said, only managing not to stumble over his words.

She peered down at the offering before her, surveying the platter; the only sign of her approval was a curt nod, which jostled her jowls. Pleased with what Harold returned with, she raised a fat arm above her head, the curtain of flab under her bicep swaying as she slid her chubby fingers against each other and produced a single piercing snap. In a moment, Daryll slunk from the crowd and delivered a polished mahogany box, the golden clasp at its front, casting a golden spark as he placed it on the table. He slid the clasp from its loop with reverence and lifted the hinged top. Inside was a collection of odd tools, and from that box, Daryll lifted a long-handled platinum mechanism. At the hinge where the two grips met was a row of spiked points. He handed this to Camilla with a low bow, that didn't seem possible for such a gargantuan man, like a squire handing the Knight he served his sword. Camilla plucked it from his hands, placed a lobster claw within it, and cracked the shell in quick, precise clamps, working her way from the base to the tip. *All this for a shell cracker?* Harold thought in disbelief.

Camilla ate with efficient and practiced motions. In a matter of silent minutes, she had cleared most of the claws. Their husked shells sucked clean by her adroit tongue and a few powerful vacuum-sucks from her mouth. She moved onto the crab legs and disposed of them in equal swiftness. All that remained was the lake of macaroni, the cheese oozing across the plate toward the edges. For the first time since she started her professional clearing of the plate, Camilla looked over to Harold.

"Harry, come sit next to me," she said while patting a handful of unoccupied inches on the hay bale next to her.

Harold stared over the table to where she indicated. There were maybe four inches of space that her hip avalanche hadn't consumed. Her body had an appetite for physical space the way her mouth did for calories, and Harold worried that he was also part of this appetite.

"There's no space left, Camilla," Harold said, hoping that would be the end of the matter. "I'll just bring my stool over," Harold stood and lifted his seat.

"No," she said. "I want you... closer," she purred in what Harold thought may have been a seductive tone, but sounded more like a gurgle. To the side, Daryll watched the exchange, his eyes darting between both sides of the table.

"Uh, Miss Coldwell, Ma'am. Maybe I can bring another hay bale over to add to your seating?" Daryll offered in a quiet, shaking voice. Camilla flicked the briefest acknowledging glance at Daryll, who loosed a yelp like a kicked dog.

"*Daryll*, are you implying that I'm too *fat* for my date to sit next to me?" her voice was as doused in venom as the cheese on her plate. Daryll's ruddy face drained all its blood and color from her question.

"N-no! I would never assume y-you were too fat—Not fat at all!" Daryll's quavering voice cut itself off in his stutters.

Harold was stupefied. *Was she insulted that Daryll called attention to her immensity? The woman who just ate an entire population of crabs and lobsters and was still prepared to hunker down on about 5 gallons of processed cheese? There's no way she isn't aware of how fat she is. Is this a chink in her armor?* He assumed she had unshakeable confidence in her size and appearance. *Can I use this somehow?* Harold stored the question for the future, and instead feared Daryll would give himself a heart attack from the stress of staring down Camilla. He seemed like a nice enough guy in Harold's eyes.

"Uh, I'm coming right over, Camilla," Harold said.

This seemed to placate her fury directed at Daryll. Her scowl flipped to a smile at Harold's acquiescence. "Lovely. Come here and help me finish this serving. My arms are so tired," she said, leaning back on her groaning seat. Her stomach's rolls, which had flopped onto the table while she ate jostled it as she shuffled her bulk to the side to make room for Harold.

"Daryll! Get me a utensil, you useless hog!" she demanded. As he rushed over to the table, he procured another enormous, ornate tool from the polished box. Camilla giggled at Daryll's obvious discomfort as he handed Harold a tool from the box that looked more like a shovel than a spoon.

"Dismissed," she said with a flap of her hand at Daryll. He nodded and shut the box, waddling off into the crowd. Camilla's eyes tracked his departure for a moment before turning their attention back to Harold, who struggled to stay balanced on the few inches afforded to him.

"Revolting, isn't it?" she asked. "Daryll, I mean. So enormous I can't fathom how he gets around," she said with a solemn shake of her head which sent her chins wobbling.

Her words confused Harold as he pushed against her oppressive hips and ass for space. *How delusional is she?* She and Daryll were so big it was hard to tell which was the fatter. *Maybe she is, considering the height difference.*

"Uh, well, some people are just bigger," he said, hoping to avoid the topic. He lifted the spoon up and stabbed into the pile of calories on her plate. *This is the weirdest date I've ever been on, hands down.* Craning the spoon to her open mouth, he tilted it down so that the pasta and cheese funneled into her mouth. She closed her eyes and moaned in ecstasy as the cheesy river flowed into her gullet.

"Mmm. You have such a gentle hand, Harry," she cooed to him. "And such a trim physique,"

"Yeah… thanks. I try to keep fit," he said as he sliced another shelf of cheese with the blade of the spoon and lifted it to her mouth, hoping it would keep her from talking. She disposed of the food like a wood chipper, and in a few grinding motions, her mouth was empty again. *I swear she just unhinged her jaw.*

"Yes, I love a nice trim body on my boys," she said while dabbing at the corners of her mouth and chins with a tablecloth. "But a *man* shouldn't be so small, don't you think? I feel like such a little piggy eating while you have had nothing," she said, clucking her tongue in chastisement.

"I don't have much of an appetite tonight," Harold countered.

"Nonsense!" she harrumphed. "Here, eat this, Harry," she said, more a command than a suggestion. Plucking the spoon from his hands, she excavated an enormous chunk from the cheese mountain. "You'll need your strength to keep up, trust me.".

"No, really. I'm fi--" his words cut off by a mouthful of cheese and shells. He choked on the spoon-bending serving she shoveled into his mouth without warning.

"That's a good boy. Eat up, darling," she said. She slid the spoon in for another, helping while placing her pudgy hand on Harold's thigh. She squeezed and rubbed his leg, getting close to his crotch while jabbing the spoon at him with her other hand.

Harold swayed in his seat, dazed. The mountain of cheese, now demolished, avalanched into his distended stomach after the force-feeding. Camilla was unrelenting, and he was on the verge of passing out from the rich cream sauce gurgling in his gullet.

"Good eating here, right, Harry? This stuff *really* sticks to the ribs," she cackled as her own gelatinous body wobbled in confirmation.

Content with her and Harold's meal, Camilla rocked herself up to her feet. She took Harold's limp arm and stuffed it into the crook of her own buttery elbow. They walked to the exit, Camilla pulling Harold along as he staggered after her. From a hidden view in the kitchens, Daryll watched them go, a deep frown creased his face.

"Oh well, he'll have fun while it lasts," he said as he pulled out his phone to check how long until his shift was over. Sliding open the screen to unlock it, Daryll looked at his phone's background with a distracted expression. It was him and Camilla, his well-defined face smiling up at the round double-chinned frown reflected by Daryll. Next to him, Camilla's narrow shoulders bookended her sharp collarbone and trim arms. "I know I did," he lamented before closing his phone's screen with a click. It was only 10, and he was closing tonight. He'd be here for hours more after the buffet-goers got their second wind.

Outside in the parking lot, Harold was getting his own second wind.

"I'm gonna call an Uber. Do you want to ride together?" he asked. Camilla smiled at him but shook her head.

"No, that's ok. I already have a car coming for me," she said as a large obsidian SUV with inky tinted windows announced itself as it crunched the pavement. The passenger window rolled down, revealing a suited man behind the wheel. He called out to Camilla.

"Come along, Miss. Coldwell. Your mother has dinner waiting," the driver said. Camilla released Harold's arm from her own and turned toward him. "Harry, I had a *very fulfilling* night with you. I'll keep in touch," she said. She took a wobbling step over to Harold and gave him a deep kiss on the mouth. The taste of salty ocean brine and processed sugar intermingled in a stomach-churning pirouette. The length of the kiss and the lingering taste left Harold gasping and gagging. As he came to his senses, Camilla had already lifted herself into the car. He watched as it whispered off into the night. Harold was at a loss as he called his own Uber home.

CHAPTER 5

The black car pulls up along the curb, slowing to a stop in a cul-de-sac. Harold is resting his head against the chill glass of the tinted window in the backseat, insensate and wordless as he has been since he left the city. He sits in the back without even recognizing his home and only leaves his daze at the sharp "KA-THUNK" of the door's power locks disengaging.

"This is you, buddy," His driver reminds him in an urging tone. No doubt wanting to get back to his own home. There's no response from Harold in the back, just his slumped form curled in the shadows. The driver angles his rearview to get a better view. The rectangular mirror frames his eyes as he stares at Harold. Still, the hard creases around them soften when he meets Harold's own haunted hollow gaze.

"Hey, bud. Y'alright? Long night, or bad night?" The older man asks. Harold looks up again, taking a molasses-slow glance out the window, and nodding to himself.

"It was... a night," Harold murmurs, his voice hollow, his eyes transfixed on some private horizon. The driver nods, familiar with his passengers becoming therapeutic clients. He twists around in his seat and pats Harold on the knee in an avuncular display of affection.

"I hear ya, pal. Date stood ya up? Listen, I know all about that. Lemme tell you a story," The old man slips the shifter into park and reaches for the ignition, prepared to kill the engine. Harold bolts up in his seat, and yanks the door open, slamming it behind him with a muffled 'thanks and goodnight.' The driver watches him stumble up to his walkway towards his front door with a smirk and knowing chortle."Gets 'em out every time," he says in a self-congratulatory way as his car whispers off into the night.

Harold stumbled through his front door, his feet knowing the path from rote mechanics seared into their fibers better than his dazed mind. His pawed at his clothes, fumbling with buttons and loops. His hands acted of their own numb accord as if they had forgotten their earlier nimble-dancing grace used to pinch and swivel the necks of wine glasses. The shed clothes trailed behind him, marking a haphazard path from the door to his bedroom. They were symbols of a life left behind, cast off like a snake slithering, sloughing, slipping out of an outgrown skin, so too had Harold undergone an incomprehensible and arcane metamorphosis throughout the night.

Nearing the end of his journey, Harold stopped at the foot of the bed, his leg jerked and kicked the final entangled remains of his designer Italian jeans. On any other night, he would fold and hang them to avoid wrinkles setting. Harold loomed over his bed in nothing but his boxers, which he pulled off with two hooked thumbs without ceremony, and then collapsed onto the bed's surface.

He lay face down, prepared to offer himself over to an insensate dreamless state. Laying there for several minutes, he rolled over, supine, groaning in frustration. Memories of the night plagued him. Flashing moments flitted through his mind, and his body responded with a mysterious yearning; but, he refused to allow his conscious self to acknowledge it. The night's events were best set to banishment within the deepest recesses where he kept memories of grade school and his first prom. To even allow a single image to penetrate from that void, to speak of the taunting thing which beckoned to him ever since he left the buffet—No!

He would not picture her—it, devouring all that fried cheese, the crumbs tumbling along like boulders in a landslide, funneled into the canyon of her cleavage. Wouldn't picture her capable fat fingers surfed on tortilla chips through the oceans of Queso Blanco dip. Or how her little pink slip of a tongue flicked out between her plush ruby red lips rubbed the rim of her mouth free of excess cream sauce. He couldn't focus on those fat little hands tunneling through the hollowed-out legs and claws of shellfish, cracking them open with startling strength, her plump palms wrapped around the lengths of their shafts with crushing power. He couldn't allow himself to imagine the plush welcoming incubation her palms would offer cradling his own shaft—NO!

Dread washes over him. He flings his eyes open and cranks his neck to survey his own body. He senses it gorging on blood and lust, feels each individual pump of the artery flooding it. Aching from its own inexhaustive greed. His penis, beyond stiff, throbbing, and filled beyond capacity like a dish sponge, struggling to soak within an ocean of primal yearning, inadequate for the task, but desperate to perish trying. Disgust and bubbling fury swells within him at the perceived disloyalty of his own biology, enough to match his penis' own ravenous craving. He'd execute his penis for treason if he were able.

Regardless of his feelings, it was impossible to ignore the blaring call to action his organ demanded. He knows this siren call will be his end, that to sail towards this lighthouse will dash his ships against the cliffs, and yet he sails onwards as his hand glides toward the coast. Without him realizing, throughout the night, something transfigured his penis into an altar of worship. A monolith carved in recognition to an alien god, an irreverent tower of devotion erected in service to a perverse foreign deity —and his goddess demanded fealty. He was a captive to soft domination, his instincts extinct.

His slithering hand snaked around his shaft, enveloping it within a white-knuckled stranglehold. Despite himself, he pumped. The motion began with his wrist, but in short order, it commissioned his entire arm for the task, incorporated into the mechanical piston which it had become. Fastened as it was to his penis, it had ceased to be a limb, and instead became an instrument of worship. Its sole purpose to pay tribute.

It felt like he was heaving an enormous weight as he massaged himself, tickled it under the collar of its engorged pink head, holding it loose at the base and cinching the pressure as he moved toward the summit. Soon he fell into a practiced rhythm. His breaths were bestial, haggard snorts and wheezing shallow pants in quick succession. In his mind, he saw Camilla's face, full and round like an overripe fruit; felt her embrace envelop him, consume him, like a wall of flesh. He could feel her flab-coated arms jiggle and crease behind closed eyes as she gripped him; her whip-smart tongue was darting and slithering up his base like the serpent along the branch to Eve; he stimulated himself in measure to the bobbing of her hips as she waddled.

His body moved of its own volition, like a mechanism being operated. He was the ghost of the machine, beholden to the operator's will, and forced to witness as his form complied. The commands from his brain were too slow, messages doomed to never arrive. Staring in horror as his hand pumped out a rhythm beyond his orchestration, he willed himself to stop, pleading, but he was in the grips of bestial function. He tried to hold it back, to contain his seed. It was impossible, like commanding lightning, not to strike. He was thrall in the grips of her stranglehold. His ejaculation was an eruption, a Judas kiss. At the point of release, he howled in abject horror, in the throes of futile rage. Waves of sensation roiled over him, emanating from the depths of his loins. Whether it was euphoria or nausea was impossible to discern. As his discharge dribbled over the tip and flowed in excess over his trembling hand, he had a single absurd thought 'My cup runneth over,' before he fell into a deep sleep.

That night he had fitful dreams. Of a carnivorous planet, it's surface an alluring utopia but concealed a hellacious being at its center, an insatiable and irresistible entity calling to him.

The next morning it branded the hellscape images on his mind. Visions of a halcyon meadow, at the center, was a tiny hill with a vibrant cherry blossom tree. The sloping tree seemed perfect to lean against and rest under its shade, but as he walked to the hill, the landscape began to shift. It was growing, rising higher, the base surging outward. Where the hill's center had been, the spot at which the tree had beckoned to him with a promise of serene respite, was now a spreading chasm, the earth's own yawning maw. An enormous gaping mouth was spreading, the tree tumbling inside the cavernous darkness, and all the while, the hill turned mountain continued to grow. He remembered turning, sprinting away. Trying to escape, but it was impossible. The slope of the mountain rose faster than his feet could carry him. He was on the base of it now, staring up at the summit blocking out the sun, casting the meadow into foreboding darkness. In the dream, he fell to his knees, then robed figures lifted him, carrying him the rest of the way. Through the mysterious omniscience of dream logic, he knew that they were cultists, worshippers of this thing which had lured him under false pretenses; and now he was their prisoner. They guided him up to the summit, his feet dragging at first, but as they closed on the summit, he walked on his own. This willing acquiescence terrified him more than any of the rest. The higher they climbed, the heat grew as did everything else, shifting from a thick humid into an acrid unbearable furnace heat.

Once they reached the summit, he understood as he stared over the crimson lipped rim into the bubbling magma-filled cauldron. With no coercion from his captors, he tumbled over into the depths but awoke before feeling the warm smothering annihilation that awaited him. He would have the dream each night for the next week, always waking with a mounting sense of disappointment at not feeling that final plunge.

ABOUT THE AUTHOR

R.G. Denbu is a debut author of SSBBW erotic short stories and novellas.

www.ingramcontent.com/pod-product-compliance
Lightning Source LLC
LaVergne TN
LVHW020543160826
845677LV00015B/4183
* 9 7 9 8 6 6 2 7 4 1 1 0 2 *